CLASSIC TAILS

The Picture of Dorian Greyhound

OSCAR WILDE
with ELIZA GARRETT

Illustrated by Pastiche Pastiche

WILDFIRE

On a warm June day, the artist Basil Basset was working in his studio, finishing a pawtrait of a young dog of extraordinary personal beauty.

'It is your best work, Basil, the best thing you have ever done,' opined Lord Henry Wooffon languidly from the divan where he lay. 'You must certainly exhibit it next year.'

'I will never display it,' the artist snuffled seriously. 'I am afraid that I have shown in it the secret of my own soul.'

Basil told Lord Wooffon about the night he became acquainted with the subject of the painting – Mr Dorian Greyhound. He was at a party, and their eyes met. Basil puffed, 'I knew that I had encountered someone so fascinating that he could absorb my whole nature, my whole soul, my very art itself.' Basil had seen Dorian every day since that night, and had produced the best work of his life.

'So why won't you exhibit his pawtrait?' asked Lord Wooffon.

'Because my heart shall be put under the world's microscope. There is too much of myself in the thing!'

Basil did not want Lord Wooffon to meet Dorian, but just as he was saying so the butler announced that Dorian Greyhound had come to the studio. Before going to receive him, Basil turned to Wooffon.

'Dorian Greyhound is my dearest friend,' he wheezed. 'He has a simple and beautiful nature. Don't spoil him. Don't try to influence him. My life as an artist depends on him. I trust you, Harry.'

'What nonsense you talk!' responded Lord Wooffon with a mirthful wag of the tail.

Dorian loped in sulkily, at first seeing only Basil. 'Oh, I am tired of sitting!' When he caught sight of Lord Henry, his ears flattened repentantly for a moment. 'I beg your pardon, Basil, I didn't know you had anyone with you!' Lord Henry introduced himself with a delicate sniff of the other's hindquarters, and Dorian, taking an immediate fancy to him, begged him to stay and talk to him while he sat. Basil reluctantly allowed it, but warned Dorian not to listen to anything Wooffon said. 'He has a very bad influence over all his chums.'

'Oh, there is no such thing as good influence, Mr Greyhound,' declared Lord Wooffon. 'Every dog must explore his own sins, and not borrow those of others.'

While Basil was deep in his work and hearing nothing of what was being said, Lord Wooffon continued to share with Dorian his philosophy on life. 'Every impulse that we strive to strangle broods in the mind, and poisons us. The only way to get rid of a temptation is to yield to it.' As he spoke Dorian stood motionless; the words of Basil's friend struck a chord deep within him.

'You have a wonderfully beautiful muzzle, Mr Greyhound. You have only a few years in which to live really, perfectly and fully, before you become hollow-cheeked, and dull-eyed, and your fur loses its lustre. Ah! realise your youth while you have it. Live! Be always searching for new sensations. There is absolutely nothing in the world but youth!'

Suddenly Basil interrupted them. 'It is finished!' he slobbered. Lord Wooffon examined it and pronounced it the finest pawtrait of modern times. 'Mr Greyhound, come and look at yourself.'

Dorian was silent at first, his eyes bright with pleasure, as the sense of his own beauty came on him like a revelation. But then a sharp pang of pain struck through him.

'How sad it is!' he murmured forlornly. 'I shall grow old, and horrible, but this picture will remain always young . . . If it were only I who was to be always young, and the picture that was to grow old! I would give my soul for that!' He threw himself on the divan, whining piteously.

Basil's tail wagged with agitation. 'This is your doing, Harry,' he harrumphed bitterly. 'Well, you have both made me hate the finest piece of work I have ever done, and I will destroy it.' He picked up the palette knife and moved towards the painting.

With a stifled yelp Dorian sprang from the couch, tore the knife from Basil's paw and flung it across the studio.

'Don't, Basil! It would be murder!' he howled. 'I am in love with it, Basil. It is part of myself.'

'Well, as soon as you are dry, you shall be varnished, and framed, and sent home,' Basil replied coldly. 'Then you can do what you like with yourself.'

The next day, Lord Wooffon called on his uncle, Lord Fourleg, to find out if he knew about Dorian's background. 'His mother was an extraordinarily beautiful pooch,' the old dog reminisced. She had disobeyed her pack and run away with a penniless young mutt, who was killed in a dogfight a few months after their marriage. Rumour had it that Margaret's father had ordered the killing, and Margaret never spoke to him again. She died within a year of giving birth to Dorian.

Wooffon thought this story made the young hound even more perfect. There was something fascinating about this pup of Love and Death. And how charming he was, with his startled eyes and jaw opened in frightened pleasure as Lord Wooffon exercised his influence over him. He decided he would seek to dominate him, and make that wonderful spirit his own.

It was a month later, while Wooffon was paying Dorian a visit at his home, that the younger dog announced that he had fallen deeply in love. 'She is an actress,' he told him, eyes burning. 'Her name is Sibyl Dane, and she is a genius.' He had come across her acting in an absurd little theatre on the grimy Isle of Dogs, and had returned every night since just to watch her perform. 'Every night she is more marvellous. She is all the great heroines of the world in one. Oh, she is the best in show!'

That night, Wooffon received word that Dorian was engaged to be married.

The following night, Dorian took his two friends to see his betrothed play Juliet. She was certainly exquisite – like a creature from a finer world. But when she performed, she was lifeless, incompetent; Dorian was silent and anxious, and his friends were horribly disappointed.

After the play, Dorian went behind the stage. Sibyl greeted him with an expression of infinite joy. 'How badly I acted tonight, Dorian!' She told him that, now she knew what life truly was, she realised the theatre was a hollow sham – and she would never act well again.

Dorian growled at her, 'You have killed my love. I wish I had never laid eyes upon you!' Sibyl's joy left her, and she trembled and whimpered – but he was unmoved, and left her there.

Dorian bounded home in a rage. As he opened the door, he suddenly caught sight of his pawtrait, which appeared to him to be a little changed. He rubbed his eyes and looked again, but the expression looked different, like there was a touch of cruelty in the mouth. He collapsed into a chair and began to think. His mind went back to his mad wish in Basil's studio, that the pawtrait might bear the burden of his passions and sins.

Surely not? And yet . . .

He resolved to resist temptation to sin from now on, to go back to Sibyl, make amends and marry her, and try to love her again. Yes, that was his duty.

He curled up in his basket and fell asleep thinking of Sibyl.

The next day, Dorian wrote a passionate letter to Sibyl, imploring her forgiveness, and accusing himself of rabid madness. But as he was writing Lord Wooffon arrived bearing some dreadful news – Sibyl had taken an overdose of dark chocolate, and killed herself!

At first Dorian was wracked with guilt. But as the minutes passed he began to muse aloud: 'So I have murdered Sibyl Dane. How extraordinarily dramatic life is!'

Henry scratched himself dismissively. 'Sibyl was of no importance; she was not even real. She withered when touched by real life, and simply passed away.'

This was enough to reassure Dorian. 'It has been a marvellous experience,' he decided. 'That is all.'

As soon as Wooffon left, Dorian hurried to the curtain screening the painting and pulled it back again. It hadn't changed any further – he knew it would have altered the moment Sibyl died. He was horrified imagining the desecration in store for the pawtrait . . . but then began to think of the pleasure there would be in watching it. He would be able to follow his mind into its secret places. What did it matter what happened to the coloured image on the canvas? He would be safe. That was everything. He pulled the curtain closed and grinned.

The next morning, Basil lumbered into Dorian's home to offer his condolences – and found the hound not remotely affected by his fiancée's suicide. He then noticed that his pawtrait was covered up, and went to remove the curtain – but Dorian rushed in front of it. 'No, Basil! I could not possibly let you see that picture.'

'You will some day, surely?'

'Never.'

'But you will sit for me again?'

'Impossible! I will come and share a chew with you. Just as pleasant.'

'Pleasanter for you, I am afraid,' murmured Basil regretfully. 'Goodbye, Dorian.'

That very day, Dorian had the painting moved to an attic room for which only he had a key. In that room, behind its curtain, the figure painted on the canvas could grow more bestial and unclean. What did it matter? No one could see it. Besides, his nature might grow finer – some love might come across his life, and purify him.

But no, that was impossible. The canvas might escape the hideousness of sin, but the hideousness of age was in store for it. The picture had to be concealed. There was no help for it.

Dorian locked the door and put the key in his pawket. He felt safe now.

When he returned downstairs he found waiting for him a little yellow book, sent over by Lord Wooffon. What was it? he wondered. He flung himself in an armchair and began to read. After a few minutes he was absorbed.

It was a poisonous book, which described within it the life of the senses – of the rejection of training and obedience, which is artificial, and the pursuit of natural rebellion, which society calls 'mischief'. It troubled one's tiny brain.

It was almost nine o'clock when Dorian finally arrived at the club and found a very bored Lord Wooffon sitting alone, idly contemplating a squeaky ball.

'It's your fault I'm late, Harry. The book you sent so fascinated me that I forgot how the time was going.'

'Yes, I thought you would like it,' replied Wooffon.

'I didn't say I liked it, Harry. I said it fascinated me. There is a great difference.'

For years, Dorian Greyhound could not – or would not – free himself from the influence of this book.

From time to time strange rumours about his life crept through the pedigreed packs of London, the most evil things against him – but his wonderful beauty never left him, so no one could believe anything to his dishonour when they saw him.

Often, after returning from one of his long periods of absence which were the source of such rumours, he would creep upstairs on spindly legs to the locked room holding a mirror, and gaze both upon his evil and ageing face on the canvas, and on the fair young snout that laughed back at him from the polished glass. He became more and more enamoured of his own beauty, more and more interested in the corruption of his own soul.

It was on the eve of Dorian's sixth birthday that Basil paid him a visit. The artist told him he was getting the midnight train to Paris, and wouldn't be returning for six months. He informed Dorian that he had been hearing the most dreadful things about him. 'Why is your friendship so fatal to young males? Why do people say that you are a dog whom no pure-minded bitch should be allowed to know? There have been stories,' Basil dribbled on, 'that you have been seen creeping at dawn out of dreadful houses and slinking into the foulest dens in London.' Basil paused and looked at Dorian mournfully. 'I wonder do I know you? I should have to see your soul. But only Dog in Heaven can do that.'

A bitter bark of mockery broke from the jaws of the younger dog. 'You shall see my soul yourself, tonight!' he snarled, seizing a lamp from the table. 'Come. You have chattered enough about corruption. Now you shall look on it snout to snout.' Basil followed Dorian upstairs, into the attic room. Dorian tore the curtain from its rod and Basil let out a yelp of horror as he saw in the dim light the hideous creature on the canvas. He recognised his brushwork, and in the left-hand corner was his own name.

'What does this mean?' he whined shrilly.

'It is the face of my soul,' Dorian growled.

Basil sank back on to his haunches. 'It's not too late, Dorian! Let us sit and pray. You have done enough evil in your life. My Dog!'

Suddenly Dorian was struck with an uncontrollable feeling of hatred for Basil, as though it had been suggested to him by the image on the canvas. He saw a knife atop a chest and seized it, before stabbing Basil over and over again!

On the pawtrait, a loathsome red dew gleamed on one of the paws, as though the canvas were sweating blood . . .

Six weeks later, Dorian went to see Lord Wooffon at his home. As his friend absent-mindedly played Poochini on the piano, Dorian told him that he was going to be good from now on. Wooffon scoffed. 'You're quite perfect. Pray, don't change.'

'And what would you say if . . . if I told you I had murdered Basil?' Dorian said, watching Wooffon intently.

'Crime belongs exclusively to the lower orders!' Wooffon barked merrily. 'No; I would imagine poor Basil fell into the Seine, and that's how he met his end. I don't think he would have done much more good work,' he sniffed. 'Recently his painting has gone off very much.'

It was a lovely night, and on his walkies home Dorian began to think over some of the things Wooffon had said to him. Was it really true that one could never change? Was there no hope for him? Ah! in what a monstrous moment of pride and passion he had prayed that the pawtrait should bear the burden of his dog days!

A new life. That was what he wanted. Surely he had begun already? Perhaps the signs of evil on the pawtrait had already gone away. He would go and look.

He entered the room and locked the door behind him, as was his custom, before flinging aside the curtain. A howl of pain and indignation broke from him. The thing was still loathsome – more loathsome, if possible, as around the jaws there was now the curved wrinkle of the hypocrite, and the blood on the paw seemed brighter. Was Basil's murder to dog him all his life?

He looked around, and saw the knife that had stabbed poor Basil Basset. As it had killed the painter, so it would kill the painter's work and all it meant! He seized the thing, and stabbed the picture with it.

The cry heard by the servants was horrible in its agony, and after receiving no reply to their urgent knocks on the door of the room, they forced it open.

When they entered they found, hanging up, a splendid pawtrait of their master as they had last seen him, in all the wonder of his exquisite youth and beauty. Lying on the floor was a dead dog, in evening dress, with a knife in his heart. He was withered, wrinkled and loathsome of visage. It was not till they had checked his collar that they recognised who it was.

THE END

First published in 2017 by WILDFIRE
an imprint of HEADLINE PUBLISHING GROUP

Illustrations copyright © Pastiche Pastiche

1

Cataloguing in Publication Data is available from the British Library

ISBN 978 1 4722 5028 5

Written by Eliza Garrett

Typeset in Perpetua

Printed and bound in Portugal by Printer Portuguesa

Headline's policy is to use papers that are natural, renewable and
recyclable products and made from wood grown in sustainable
forests. The logging and manufacturing processes are expected to
conform to the environmental regulations of the country of origin.

HEADLINE PUBLISHING GROUP
An Hachette UK Company
Carmelite House
50 Victoria Embankment
London EC4Y 0DZ

www.headline.co.uk
www.hachette.co.uk

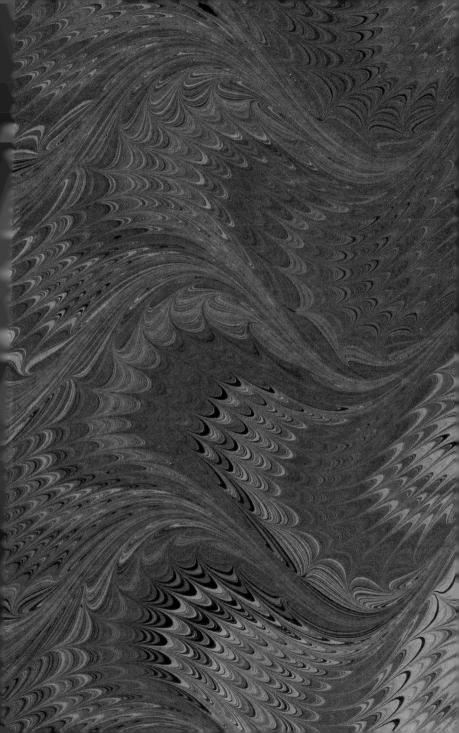